BUNNY
WILL NOT
JUMP!

**WRITTEN AND ILLUSTRATED
BY JASON THARP**

Ready-to-Read

Simon Spotlight
New York   London   Toronto   Syd

SIMON SPOTLIGHT

An imprint of Simon & Schuster Children's Publishing Division

1230 Avenue of the Americas, New York, New York 10020

This Simon Spotlight edition December 2020

Copyright © 2020 by Jason Tharp

All rights reserved, including the right of reproduction in whole or in part in any form.

SIMON SPOTLIGHT, READY-TO-READ, and colophon are registered trademarks of Simon & Schuster, Inc.

For information about special discounts for bulk purchases, please contact Simon & Schuster Special Sales at 1-866-506-1949 or business@simonandschuster.com.

Manufactured in the United States of America 1020 LAK

10 9 8 7 6 5 4 3 2 1

This book has been cataloged with the Library of Congress.

ISBN 978-1-5344-8303-3 (hc)

ISBN 978-1-5344-8302-6 (pbk)

ISBN 978-1-5344-8304-0 (eBook)

He seems sad, too.

I just want him to be happy.

Maybe you can help!

It all started the other day. . . .

I wonder which one of us can jump farthest.
Okay. I will try my best.
Great! One, two, three . . . jump!

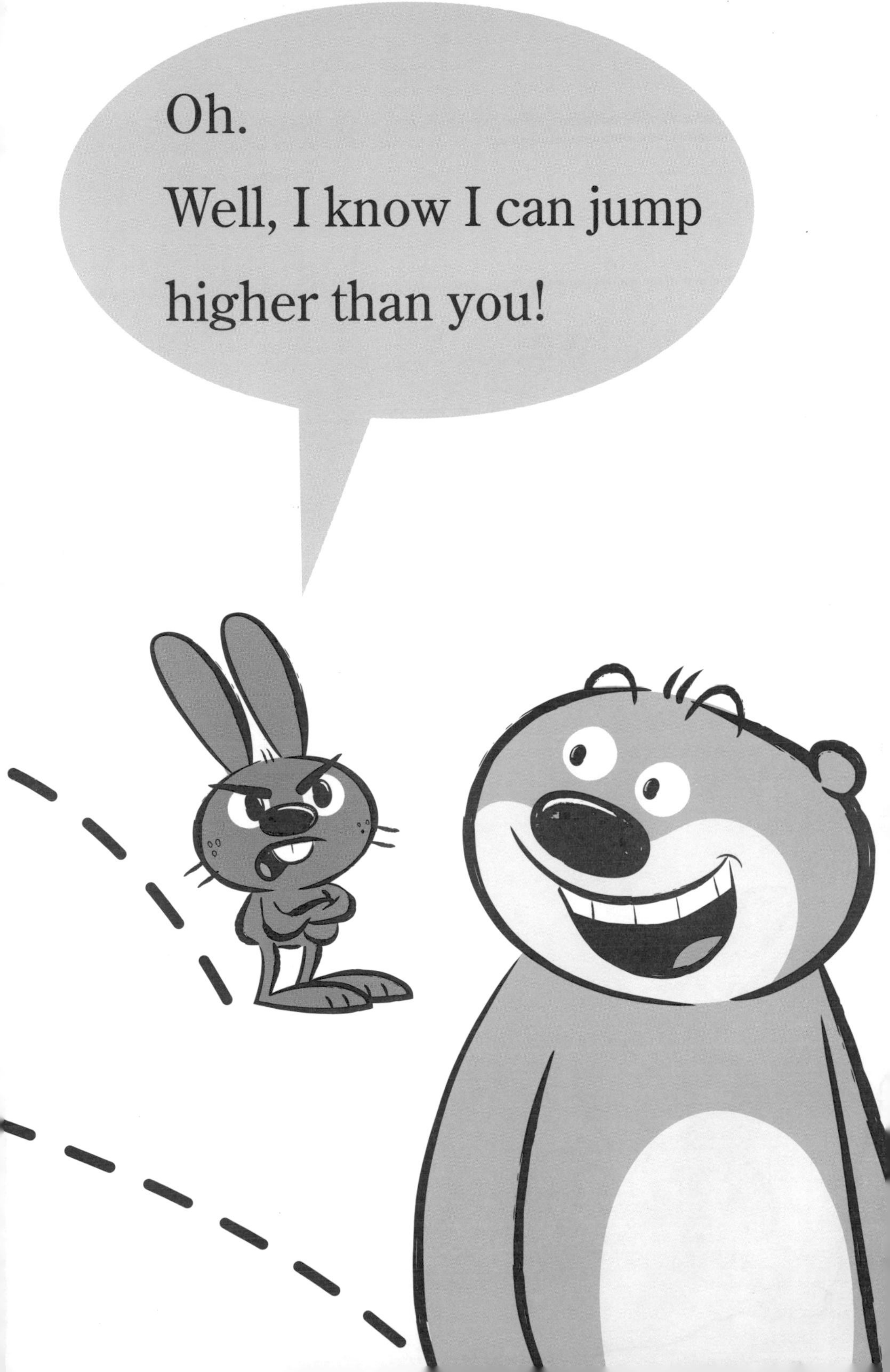
Oh.
Well, I know I can jump
higher than you!

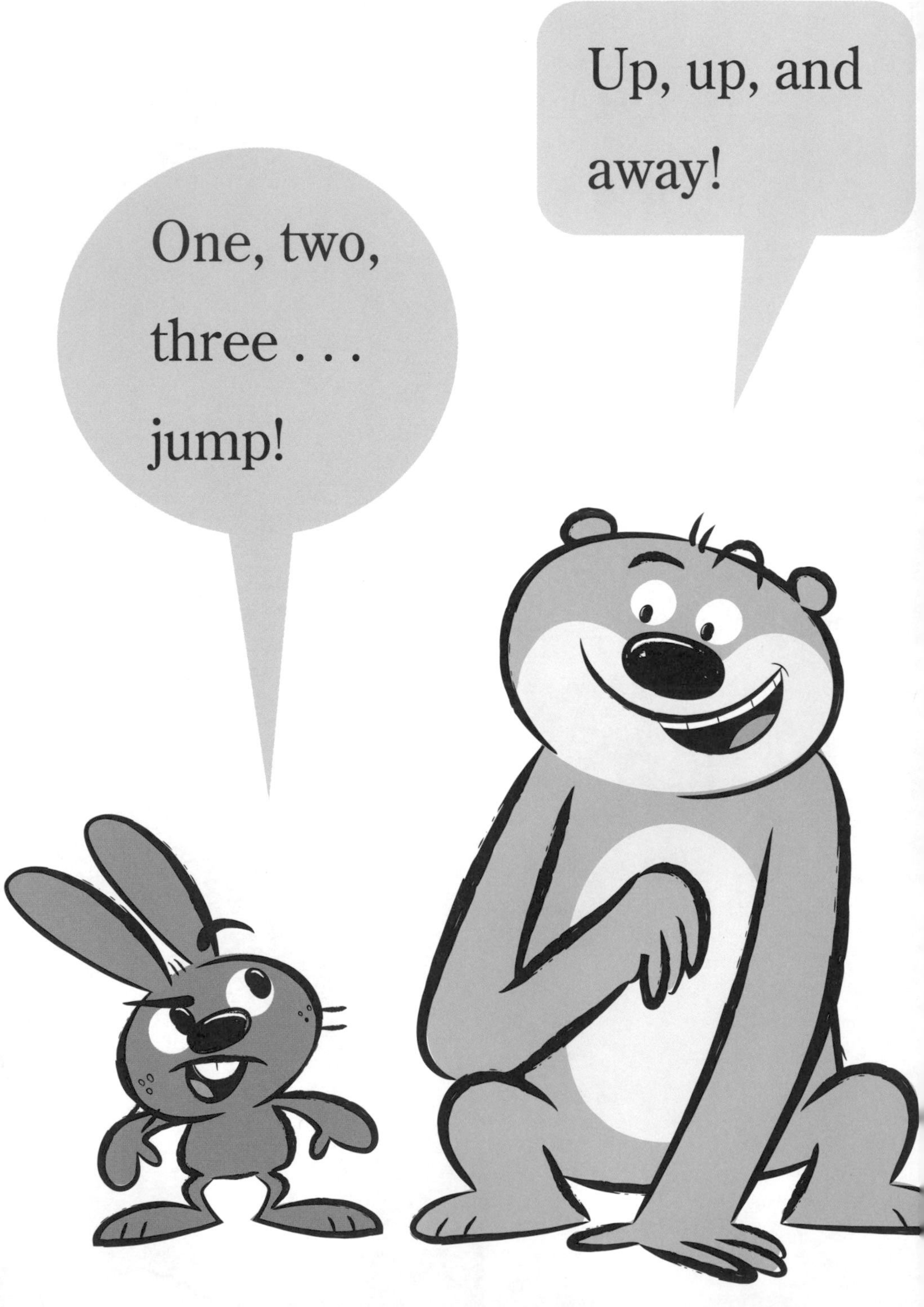
One, two, three . . . jump!
Up, up, and away!

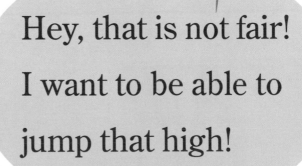

Hey, that is not fair! I want to be able to jump that high!

It is okay, Bunny.
Jumping makes you happy.
I think if you try again,
you will love it.

What is the point?
I will never be able to
jump like you.

Now Bunny will not jump at all!
I told him I would give him
a HUGE prize if he jumped.

I even tried to make him jump by scaring him.

Boo!

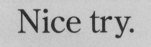

Bunny still will not jump.

That is why I need your help.

Maybe if you shake the book,

Bunny will jump!

Ready? Okay!
Please shake the book
up and down . . .
now!

That made me dizzy,
but it did not make
me jump.

It did not work, but that is okay.

We can try again.

This is the Jump-O-Matic 4000.

It is a machine that will help Bunny jump.

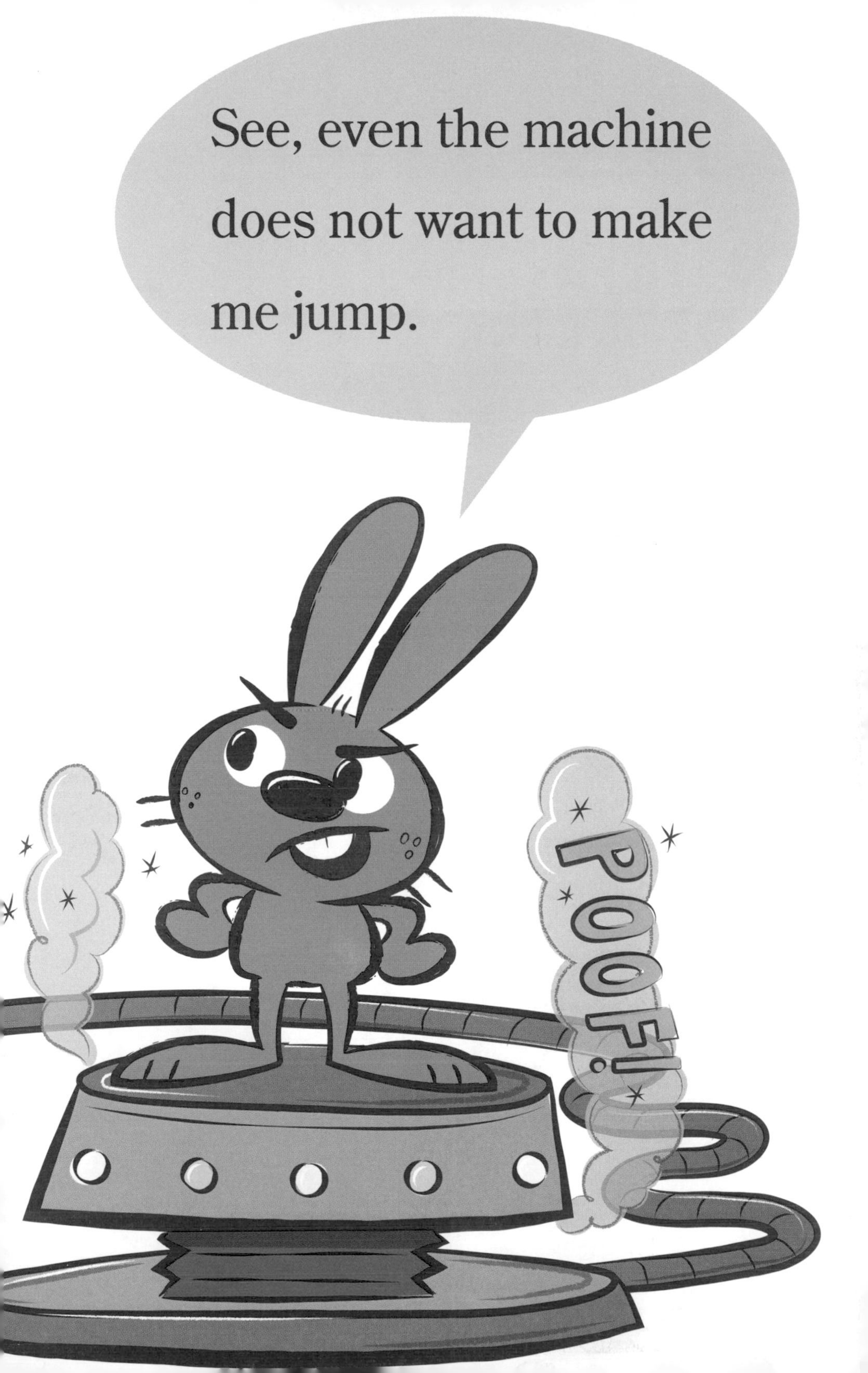
See, even the machine does not want to make me jump.
POOF!

I do not understand.
I am a bunny.
I should be the best
at jumping!

You are great at jumping.
I can jump higher and farther
because I am taller.
We are different,
and that is okay!

Besides, it is not about
being like me.
It is about having fun!
Just try one time?

Come on, Bunny.
Do not think about how I jump.
Jump the best way YOU can jump!

Flip the page back and forth
to help Bunny jump! ➡